ALSO BY LAI

CW00350878

STOP IT! It is all in your head

The RULE BOOK to Smash The infamous glass ceiling - For women & young women everywhere - personal transformation & success 101.

The Think, Look & Act The Part Series.

Think The Part

Upgrade your consciousness and mind-set. Make winning a key part of your life and business.

Look The Part

Upgrade your personal brand. Make presenting your unique Best Self a key part of your life and business.

Act The Part

A personal coach to act in spite of fear, right here, right now.

More non-fiction books and courses are coming soon. Keep an eye for new releases, giveaways and pre-release specials by checking at www.thepeoplealchemist.com

You can also buy my books and courses directly from the author at

www.payhip.com/LauraMariani

ABOUT THE AUTHOR

Laura Mariani is an Author, Speaker and Entrepreneur.

She started her consulting business after a successful career as Senior HR Director within global brands in FMCG, Retail, Media and Pharma.

Laura is incredibly passionate about helping other women to break through barriers limiting their personal and/or professional fulfilment. Her best selling nonfiction *STOP IT! It is all in your head* and the *THINK, LOOK & ACT THE PART* series have been described as success and transformation 101.

She is a Fellow of the Chartered Institute of Personnel & Development (FCIPD), Fellow of the Australian Human Resources Institute (FAHRI), Fellow of the Institute of Leadership & Management (FInstLM), Member of the Society of Human Resources Management (SHRM) and Member of the Change Institute.

She is based in London, England with a strong penchant for travel and visiting new places. She is a food lover, ballet fanatic, passionate about music, art, theatre. She likes painting and drawing (for self-expression not selling but hey, you never know…), tennis, rugby, and of course fashion (the Pope is Catholic after all).

www.thepeoplealchemist.com
@PeopleAlchemist
instagram.com/lauramariani_author

ThePeopleAlchemist Press publishes self help, inspirational and transformational books, resources and products to help #TheWomanAlchemist in every woman to change her life/ career and transmute any circumstance into gold, a bit like magic to **Unlock Ignite Transform.**

ISBN: 978-1-7398293-1-5

"The pint size village made her feel even smaller, the beach and the coastline the only relief. Ah, she loved being by the sea …"

GABRIELLE

FROM THE DIARY OF

LAURA MARIANI

THE PEOPLE ALCHEMIST

Your life can change at any point in time. You just need to decide who you want to be, what you want do or have. And just like that, everything changes …

"I BLINKED MY EYES AND IN AN INSTANT,
DECADES HAD PASSED."
— JOHN MARK GREEN

GABRIELLE

PROLOGUE

Time is passing by relentlessly. Time past, time present, time future.

But this main fundamental of physical reality is not what it seems: it's an optical illusion.

What physicists tell us is that things, in the quantum world, do not happen in linear steps. They happen now. But you are only aware of the reality you choose to observe.

Consciousness itself creates the material world. The linear passing of time in stark contrast with the seemingly random crossing of time in our consciousness.

A constant stream of consciousness.

Everything is NOW - the constant flow connected by some force within each person. And memories provide a constant connection to events, places and people.

There are infinite possibilities that the world can offer at every moment .

And just like that, one day, everything can change ...

GABRIELLE

G abrielle woke up, the overnight video still playing on her IPad.

"I am a Goddess, I am a Queen ... I am valued ... if I want it, I got it".

The rain was falling thick and fast. You could smell it in the air. Boy it was noisy: the thunder, the rain ... It was so dark, winter is definitely coming.

"What day is it?" They all feel the same right now. Nowhere to go, nothing to do, nobody to see. Oh yes, it's Saturday. Who cares? Does it really make a difference?

"Keeping a routine gives me some parvence of normality, for myself really. Glowing up for myself so to speak, self-discipline is self-love someone said".

. . .

Yes, but sometimes though it's such a drag...

The overnight video with looped affirmations was a bit of a thing to get used to: it kept waking her up during the night - maybe it was the glare of the screen or maybe the subconscious resistance. Anyhow, she got used to it eventually and now she can sleep for the entire night.

"This time is working for me ... re-wiring, reconstructing".

Gabrielle thought how everything had changed one day, just like that.

It's amazing how life can turn just in a second. Uncontrollably. All the things you always wanted to do on pause. Until someone else decides to press the play button again.

It is easier to think that way somehow - an external force controlling your life, stopping you from achieving all the things you've always wanted to do, being the amazing being you always believed you were going to be. Funny.

Tomorrow, always longing for tomorrow, whereas everything in you ought to reject it. Suddenly, there almost wasn't a tomorrow.

To be fair, she enjoyed the alone time. She had always been a loner: as child lost in her books, as an adult chasing the next win in the never-ending climb. She had cancelled many events before, dates, and meetings with friends at the last minute. There was always tomorrow. There was always something more important to do.

· · ·

People were amazed by her unwavering confidence, her strength, they looked up to her like some sort of Wonder Woman.

"Mirror, Mirror of them all, Who's the fairest of them all?"

Sometimes she just didn't feel too good about herself and pretending was just too strenuous. It was exhausting, draining.

Now, there's no need to make up excuses.

Lockdown has been good for her, some time to focus on herself with little distraction. Getting to know who Gabrielle actually is or wants to be. Getting to like this Gabrielle, perhaps even love. And level up.

She looked out of the window, Canonbury Square Gardens; the rain was coming down incessantly.

"I love this area of London, George Orwell lived in the square somewhere, I think", many significant figures from the arts and literary worlds have lived in the square. That was part of the appeal when she moved three years ago, the last move in the climb - the listed Georgian townhouse.

The outdoor seating are engraved with names of people who had lived in the square. A physical token or memories always present.

IN MEMORY OF EDDIE AND MABEL WALTERS WHO LIVED IN
CANONBURY SQUARE

On a *normal* Saturday she would have popped in at The Estorick and looked at the latest exhibition, got lost in the surrounding, feasting her eyes, feeding the soul.

Perhaps bring her coffee in the Square Gardens; there are always people there.

The Friends of Canonbury Square volunteers do such a good job keeping the gardens so clean, so neat.

"What time is it? Definitely coffee time. One needs coffee to meditate".

Gabrielle loved the smell of the coffee permeating the house, slowly but surely, a ripple effect, a sinuous wave propagating everywhere. Gabrielle made her bed first: someone somewhere said all successful entrepreneurs do so, the first task of the day-accomplished sort of thing. Much easier not to, but she did it anyway. Bed done. Coffee ready.

"Time for meditation now".

She had tried complete silence before but found that guided meditation was somehow easier. Someone, something to help with the ever-wondering thoughts going through her mind. But she found mantra meditation even better. The relentless repetition of the same words has a reassuring, calming, almost numbing effect on her. Something to focus for ten minutes or so.

"Getting good with these tapes" she reassured herself.

"I think I'll light up a candle to get me in the mood".

· · ·

The flickering light in the dark room, thunder and the pitter platter of the rain against the window was playing in the background: she sat down, crossed legged.

"Tell me again why oh why do people sit down cross legged to meditate?". She asked herself. She always got cramps. And always in the same foot which then goes numb.

She did it anyway. OK, here we go....

"Shreem Brzee, Shreem Brzee, Shreem, Brzee," Dr Pillai was chanting and Gabrielle repeated along. Out loud.

"108 times are a lot of times to repeat out loud".

Stop. Focus.

"Shreem Brzee, Shreem Brzee..." sip of coffee, "Shreem Brzee, Shreem Brzee..." rambles, rambles. Boom.

Bang! I think the neighbors are going for their daily walk, their door as loud as they are.

"Shreem Brzee, Shreem Brzee"... My daily walk is out of the question for now.

She found peace of mind in walking – not a surprise there as she always really enjoyed it. The pandemic gave Gabrielle a new, more in-depth appreciation of being out there, alone, in gratitude for life. Appreciating everything that she's so lucky to be able to experience.

. . .

However, there's a limit: as much as she loved it, she didn't quite like getting soaked. People who golf don't seem to mind the rain.

"I'm not one of those" said Gabrielle "I love being by the water, just not drenched in it".

She always loved the smell of water, such a sense of peace and tranquility. She grew up by the water.

Angel Canal is a great place for long walks, she thought. The sunshine peeking through the clouds, the water moving with the breeze glistening like a dance.

"Shreem Brzee ... Shreem Brzee".

At the weekend it's usually hustle and bustle, full of city professionals sipping their dairy free latte whilst sending the last email before enjoying the weekend.

Not now.

Now she has the canal almost to herself. It was odd. The water moving, steadily continuously, rocking the boats like a lullaby, the sun capturing the movements.

"Isn't it wonderful?"

The boats look restless and so does she.

C-O-N-C-E-N-T-R-A-T-E.

"Shreem Brzee, Shreem Brzee ... Shreem Brzee ".

. . .

"How long is left now", Gabrielle peaked at the YouTube video playing, "another few minutes. Never realised ten minutes is such a long time".

Concentrate Gabri.

"Shreem Brzee ... Shreem Brzee",107, "Shreem Brzee".
   Namaste, meditation done.

Damn, the coffee is cold now. I'll make another before I start with my morning pages. Gabrielle started free writing journaling at the beginning of the first lockdown. Outpouring of unrestrained consciousness on a page, unbridled confessions or better still, therapy, but free. Julia says it should be done first thing in the morning, without fail, before the conscious mind takes over, AND for at least three pages.

Some days, it was difficult enough to write even one. Some days, Gabrielle could write forever. She was never one to keep a diary. But this, she learned to enjoy, eventually, and stuck with it. It's amazing what comes up sometime when you start writing.

BY HAND.

The movement of the pen along the paper, accompanying the free stream of uncensored thoughts is therapy in itself. She wasn't used to writing by hand anymore. Her handwriting was illegible sometimes. Heck not great grammar either, there is no auto-correct spelling. But that is the point of morning pages: to free the mind up from the ever-present Inner Critic, and let it flow. The future becomes the present, becomes the past, and becomes the present.

"Who writes by hand anymore?" she thought holding the hot steaming bowl.

Gabrielle sat in the small alcove by the window looking at the rain falling down, fresh coffee on the side table, notebook on her lap and started writing.

DEAR DIARY,

Why oh why did I write that? It feels like being a teenager again, even worse being back at school. Yuck, couldn't have picked a worst time. Much of it thankfully is a blur - a purposeful blur, a closed door behind, never to be reopened.

Why is it coming up now? Go away. GO AWAY.

But the pen kept going, unwavering ... And so Gabrielle kept writing ...

Why are girls always so mean? To other girls I mean.

"Gabri, why don't you go and mix with the other girls?", the teacher was trying to move her along as she was talking to *maman*.

"Gabrielle is not mixing very well, Mrs. Arkin. Don't get

me wrong, her grades are really good, it's the social interactions that are lacking".

Mean, mean, mean. Secondary school - a random assembly of hormonal humans trying to assert their identity - is a recipe for disaster. Give me a book and paint brushes anytime, they beat people 100 to 1.

Ugh. Secondary school and living in a small village. The quintessential village with thousand Hyacinths Bucket, pardon Bouquet.

A deadly combination.

NOTHING GOOD COMES OUT OF VILLAGES EITHER,
IT IS ALWAYS THE SAME THING:
"*BLACKMAIL, SEXUAL DEVIANCE, SUICIDE, AND MURDER*" -
INSPECTOR BARNABY.

"Gabri, why are you dressed like that? Gabri, what would Mrs. So and So think,

Gabri, you can't do that, Gabri, are you listening?".

"You need to look your best Gabri, it is better to be envied than to be pitied".

There must be more to life than this. She wanted to show them all.

. . .

"I'm strong, I'm smart, I don't need anybody, and I can do it. I'll show them", she kept repeating to herself.

The pint size village made her feel even smaller, the beach and the coastline the only relief. Ah , she loved being by the sea, she could sit pondering for hours.

So free, so calm, majestic and devastatingly strong. Full of hidden treasures.

She wanted to be like the ocean. Free and majestic, strong.

Free. Climbing the corporate ladder. Strong. Career was always something she aspired to, being at the top, no matter what, no matter where, being the best. Rich and successful of course.

One day she knew she was going to be.

Gabrielle had wanted to escape as fast as she could. She always knew she wanted to leave. Escape from Alcatraz, or at least that's how it felt.

And she did.

"Gabri, you are going to be alone in London. What happens if you are sick? What if you can't find a job?" her mother was having a fit.

"I'll survive ma".

"You can always come back home, you know".

She was determined not to. Failure was never an option.

· · ·

As she was boarding the train to London with all her belongings crammed in a couple of suitcases, she knew it was the right decision.

Her parents had come to say goodbye, her mother crying of course.

The dispatcher blew the whistle, it was time to go.

One last hug.

The train started moving faster and faster, and faster. The village quickly fading behind her, she felt the invisible shackles loosening. Slowly. She felt lighter. Her nose was pressed against the cold window, soaking every bit of the new views.

Arriving in London was like shredding too tight-fitting skin. Just like that, everything changed - she was now wearing a new one.

Nobody really cares or knows who you are and what you do here. That's part of its appeal: the beauty of living in total solitude and anonymity amongst millions of people.

A few hours journey but a million miles apart.

"Funny" she thought.

"Victoria Station" announced the conductor.

Gabrielle looked at her belongings: she packed light, minimal luggage to start afresh. The heavier baggage wasn't evident to her yet.

· · ·

She stepped into the platform, her feet firmly on the ground.

The main roof of Victoria station glinting in the lunchtime sun, its slopes covering an area equivalent to three football pitches. It was one o'clock and the station was jammed packed with people zig zagging each other.

"Hey, lady, watch where you are going!"

"Sorry" she responded. Gabrielle joined the long queue in the black taxi rack outside the station.
    "Hello love".

"Camden Passage, Islington, please" Gabrielle said to the taxi driver.
    Here we go.

Her first *bijou* apartment in London, estate agents speak for a studio flat where you can't even swing a cat. She loved it. It was just above Decadent Vintage, one of the many shops in the passage. She bought her first vintage Dior there.

In the first months when she first moved in, she sat for hours by the window watching the world go by: the weekend bargain hunters, the antique market, the hustle and bustle of restaurants, cafes and market stalls. The outsider looking in.

.   .   .

She loved browsing through the fashionable contemporary clothing, modern designer jewellery, Japanese art prints, together with specialist antique, silver ware, vintage clothing. The retro shops provided the backdrop for market stalls selling affordable collectables, vintage clothes and *objets d'art* that find their way into antique shops and homes all over the world. What's not to love?

She even loved the daily noise coming out of the Camden Head and its free comedy club, seven nights a week.

Gabrielle still enjoys the occasional shopping spree there: some British and international artisan cheeses at Pistachio & Pickle Dairy and the artisanal chocolates at Paul A. Young.

"I wonder when the shops will open again," she said.
     "Funny " she had been carrying the "village" of old structures around for the last twenty years. Rules, beliefs, way of seeing and doing things the proper way".

Breaking the glass ceiling had been actually easier than breaking her own: the invisible ceiling in her head, the internal set point that reminded her what "her place" was.

Success, money, income, all a symbolic reflection of beliefs about personal and professional market value. And what socioeconomic class you are in. Or trying to be in.

Shopping, yes shopping too ...

. . .

The first time Gabrielle brought home a brand new Chanel bag was like taking home a brand new baby, the fruit of your hard labour and love.

Walking into the Chanel boutique in new Bond Street was like a dream: the plush and pristine environment, the sophisticated smell, the sales associates a populist version of Chanel mannequins.

I can't believe handbags smell. But they do. I still remember the subtle unmistakable waft of calf leather when the associate opened THE box of a brand new 11.12; the double clasp, the interlaced metal chain and leather, the diamond quilting, the softness yet sturdiness of the leather. It represents so much more than a bag. Look at me, look at what I've become.

"I'll get this," she said, handing over her credit card. She did that without asking for the price. Gabrielle walked out of the boutique with her feet barely touching the ground, almost skipping. The exhilaration of that purchase was like a potent drug, the high overpoweringly seductive.

But with every high there is a low, and the need for one more fix.

"God, I had a few". Fixes. Chanel, LVs, Prada, Louboutins. Each time the high was lower, and each time the effect was briefer.

And now they are all sitting in pretty boxes in the

wardrobe.

It has been a time of forced simplicity; you could say Covid-19 has taught us how to pare back and reconnect with the things that really count. Who would have thought we didn't need to buy that many bags or shoes?! Go figure!

Sitting in pajama on zoom calls somehow you don't need that much. Just need to remember not to stand up too hastily when the camera is on.

NOTE TO SELF: THE CAMERA IS ON,
KNICKERS ON SCREEN NOT A GOOD LOOK

Just like that, everything had changed. Everything that was so important, not as important any more.

Was it ever?

Symbols, worth, survival: feelings powering actions.

The Working-Class Millionaire worked very hard for his money. I guessed when he started to earn more than his inner worth set point he had to work harder. Longer hours. Or somehow sacrifice more to make it feel fair.

That was one of the first things he ever told her when they first met.

"He is a m-i-l-l-i-o-n-a-i-r-e" his mouth filling up.

How much money he makes, how much everything he owes costs. That made Gabrielle cringe, so *déclassé.*

. . .

He was constantly trying to surpass his father, a working class immigrant who made a fortune post war. Never actually believed he could.

She could never understand at the time how an investment banker had such an aversion to money and being wealthy.

He never quite adapted to his new habitat.

The concert had just ended and the foyer was buzzing, all talking about the amazing performance. Gabrielle herself was still euphoric from it. Beethoven's 9th symphony had this effect on her, lifting her spirit and soul to a higher place.

She admired the incredible artistry and skill of the orchestra but mostly, she was flooded with emotions. Not usual for her, passion requires vulnerability and we can't show weakness, can we?

"So what did you think? Did you like it?" Gabrielle asked the Working-class Millionaire.

"I'd rather have my eyes scratched with a needle".

"Pardon?" Gabrielle turned her head slightly.

"I didn't grow up with this music, it doesn't do anything for me. It is music for pansy people".

. . .

"Not many people grow up listening to Beethoven or classical music on a daily basis. Nevertheless, you can't deny how magnificent it is. Even more so as Beethoven was deaf when he composed it".

"That figures, it sounded like it".
    I can just hear it now, was he serious?

The crowd proceeded slowly toward the exit of the Barbican Centre, hurrying them along Silk Street.
    As they walked hand in hand they couldn't have been more apart. Gabrielle was for once glad to be amongst so many people.

As much as Gabrielle wanted to leave her past behind her once and for all, he was clinging to it, carrying it with him wherever he went. Where and how he grew up defined him like an indelible mark.
    Gabrielle was always striving to improve and that attitude was inconceivable for her.
    She couldn't quite understand how one would want to remain a moth instead of becoming a butterfly.

Gabrielle had risen to the top of the corporate ladder and was enjoying every minute of it. Mr. Working Class Millionaire had to go.

. . .

The Stud was tall, muscular with deep green eyes and voluptuous lips, which he knew how to use perfectly: the spark between them was instant, from the moment they met.

The way he looked at her made her feel like the most beautiful and desired woman in the world. The fact that he was several years younger than she was made it all even more exciting, talking about men-in-power-with younger totty in tow. Except this time, she was the one in power and the man was the totty.

God, sex was good. I wonder why I thought about that now. Must be the rain, it always puts me in the mood.

The thrill coupled with the validation was a potent aphrodisiac - the gentle stroking of the ego in between the gentle stroking of the nipples.

As an introvert, Gabrielle was generally happy on her own – the pandemic made her miss-doing things with other people (shocking). One of those is definitely sex. Self-love works only for a while...

Their first time was in a hotel room at a Company conference. The hide and seek, the sneaking around added to the thrill. Their public professional relationship giving way to a steamy and passionate relationship in private. Secret sex, secret encounters, a relationship hidden from the world.

And at the beginning it was fun, exciting but after a while it became tedious; she wanted a proper relationship - who wants to spend every weekend alone?

"I should have known, all the signs were there and I ignored them".

Something was always happening at the weekend, she confronted him once and asked him outright if he was having an affair.

"How can you say that?" The Stud said, and he then started crying.

Seriously?

A cancer survivor in remission, he was getting anxious each time his check up was coming closer, or his mum called (I suppose that's what you get when you go out with boys). However big or small, there was always something happening at the weekend.

Blah blah ... blah blah ... blah blah blah.

"God, I sound like a real bitch here".

His cancer was his Linus blanket. Gabrielle had thought of leaving him so many times and each time the sob story would come out and so she stayed. She didn't want to be the heartless cow that left him when he was down in the dumps, depressed. Should have.

NOTE TO SELF: ALWAYS LISTEN TO INSTINCT

Six months after they finally split, she came across a charity website and there it was: a picture of a couple who had a very successful fundraising event - The Stud and his girlfriend. The problem was that the fundraising event took place when they were still together.

•   •   •

"WE were together, not THEM".

An affair my ass! I WAS THE OTHER WOMAN!
Fierce competition for jobs is one thing but this, this went against all her principles.

Gabrielle felt sick, literally S-I-C-K.
She sat in her bath and scrubbed and scrubbed and scrubbed for hours and hours until she felt clean and remotely better.
She was so mad, she even dreamt of killing him a few times in the most painful way (note to self, plot for a book) and in the slowest way possible (book series). Then downgraded it to chopping his dick off.

"That could do".

"I guess a twatt with cancer is still a twatt".

She took her bowl of coffee and sat there, resting her hand for a minute. The men in her life had been a projection of her inner thoughts, beliefs and perception.
What she always thought was an outer game was really far more an inner game. This was never more apparent than when she met The QC.

Gabrielle had spent her morning perusing Islington Farmer Market, on Chapel Market, looking for a variety of fresh produce, local delicacies and organic foods.

Then a bit of window-shopping at Little Paris to look at some eclectic range of vintage, curiosities, contemporary fashion and home accessories directly sourced from France. She was nervous thinking about tonight, for the first time in a long time.

"This one could be good".

She amused herself with a spot of lunch at Salut , in Essex Road.

Islington residents are spoiled with the local food scene, with very few areas offering so many restaurants and so many great places to eat and Gabrielle's love for food was fully indulged.

She loved Salut's open kitchen, watching the chefs creating the magic - local produced meat, sustainably sourced fish, and organic vegetables all mixed with incredible passion.

The food was wonderful, the portions on the small side but completely worth it. The atmosphere intimate & friendly.
She chose the Pan-Fried Scallops, Pig's Trotter & Green Apple Declination.
Just a starter.
She didn't want to feel too full, or look bloated: the dress she was going to wear was not very forgiving.

"Time seems to go so slowly today".

. . .

"Why is it that sometimes months go by like days and hours feel like months?"

A long shower to freshen up and then she could start getting ready. It was three o'clock now and her date was at seven.

"God, another four hours".

She took her time to get ready. Dressing up, but not too much. Sexy, but not too much. Fitting for Sunday evening drinks. Just a touch of red lipstick in an otherwise almost make-up free face to show a bit of effort. But not too much.

"I am naturally this beautiful, right?!"

Five o'clock.

A lot of time.

Six o'clock.

Spritz of perfume.

Six thirty.

Gabrielle started to leave the house. A last glance at the mirror to check everything was as supposed to. Her sleeveless black dress, just above the knee, revealed enough of her slim but curvy figure and her long slender legs. The knee-high boots complemented the look perfectly.

She waved her hand at a black taxi passing by "Knightsbridge, The Mandarin Oriental, please", Gabrielle said to the driver.

As they arrived the porter opened the taxi door.

"The bar please".

"Turn right there on the left, ma'am".

Ma'am??? God did I look that old Gabrielle thought? Never mind.

The bar was dark, atmospheric, an intimate setting, as if it had purposely staged for romantic rendezvous. A few couples were sitting here and there, enjoying drinks and nibbles. One man was sitting at the bar, alone. He turned his head, as if he knew she was arriving and then smiled, pleased with what he saw.

And so was she. The QC was just like his picture. Authoritative, distinguished and masculine.

He stood up and greeted her warmly (thank God he was tall), a kiss on each cheek, "You smell amazing" he said as he was *breathing* her in.

He ordered some bubbly. Nice taste. Gabrielle loved bubbly. Expensive one. She chooses to drink it often, not just on special occasions, a signal to others that her whole life is a special occasion, someone who stands on the outside of crowds.

For a first date everything seemed to go amazingly well; the conversation was flowing, flirtation and banter with the occasional casual touch.

When she first saw his profile on the Encounters Dating site without a picture, she was dubious. Mind she didn't put up a picture either, but that was different.

"I don't really want everybody to know my private business or being recognised", he had said, "I am a very public figure".

They exchanged numbers and pictures quickly, and he disclosed his full name and the website link for his Chamber so she could Google him. What were we doing before Google, God knows.

She googled him all right: divorced three times, made Silk in 1999, endless landmark cases won around the world. Described as a genius.

The famous QC. Perfect.

"What are you looking for?" he asked.

"Someone smart that I can talk to about anything and everything. Someone attractive and by that I mean that I am attracted to. Someone who has his life figured out, I don't want a rescue project. And someone who has bigger balls than I have. Definitely. I want to be the girl in a relationship".

She regretted saying that as soon as she said it.

He nodded and waved his finger in the air: "Tick, tick, tick. Three out of four isn't bad".

"Which three?" and they both smiled.

"I like you. I feel like kissing you".

Did he just blush saying that? Gabrielle looked closely. Perhaps it's just the lights in the room. Nope, he was definitely blushing.

"Why don't you?" Gabrielle hinted. He leaned forward and kissed her gently on the cheek.

"Listen, I wasn't expecting this date to go on for too long. For a first date, I normally schedule half an hour or so. You know, just an introductory first drink".

. . .

SCHEDULE???

"But now, I don't want it to end, I'm having too much fun. I'm hungry though. I was going to stop at Waitrose, get a couple of steaks and then watch Downton. Care to join me? I would love that".

Wait, did the QC just say he is watching Downton Abbey?

"At your house, you cooking..."

"Yes", he said.

"Can you cook? I mean, has anyone eaten your food and is still living? And talking to you?"

"Cheeky. Steak, salad and glass of red. Or two. I promise I will be on my very best behavior".

Gabrielle thought how crazy that was, she had only just met him, a complete stranger, but she felt safe, totally comfortable.

"I can't believe I did that, the irresponsibility of youth" she reflected. She'd be horrified today if her niece did that.

They arrived at his house in South Kensington; actually mansion is a far more fitting description. Everything was just as she imagined: a fabulous open plan Boffi kitchen with quartz worktops, Gaggenau appliances and glass sliding doors leading to a show stopping west facing garden with

Japanese maple tree, patio heaters and built in seating, marble bathrooms, wooden flooring, air conditioning, inbuilt smart TVs, electric blinds, under floor heating and security system.

"I sound like an estate agent here. How odd that I remember that".

The evening went by far too fast and, when it was time to leave, he called her a taxi.

"Islington please", and quickly handed the fare to the driver, the perfect old fashioned gentleman "make sure she gets home safe".

"Yes sir".

"Text me when you get home". And so she did.

The QC was absolutely brilliant and Gabrielle enjoyed the long debates they had. She was proud he was comfortable talking about his cases and asked her opinion. Made her feel really good about herself. On par.

His mind was absolutely mesmerising. His ego however was ginormous and he was unequivocally self-centered. A man used to live life on his own terms with people around him accommodating every single one of his whims.

That's how Gabriele liked it too. It was unbearable. Mostly because it was like looking in a mirror and not quite liking what you see.

. . .

He was leaving for Hong Kong in a few days, a very important case. Everything he did was always *very important.*

"Come tonight, I want to see you".

He was going for a couple of months and she was going to miss him.

She could have easily got dressed and gone to spend time with him. But she was ready for the night, face off.

"He's f***ing unbelievable," she thought, "how dare he? Does he think I do not have commitments?"

She didn't go. And just like that everything changed.

It was the beginning of the end. Everything that could have been and never was.

Looking at yourself in the mirror and liking what you see is much harder than one thinks. Looking at yourself in the mirror and loving what you see even harder. Perfection is so hard to achieve and trying to be perfect all the time is exhausting.

Always striving, never arriving. Like the Champagne Socialist: working class, uber gifted, scholarship for Eton, EVP in one of the Big 4 consulting firms and still suffering from Impostor Syndrome.

Gabrielle met her Italian friend Paola for a spot of lunch at Trullo, a lovely tiny restaurant just around Highbury Corner, in St. Paul's Road.

Food, wine, attention to detail – Trullo is a neighbourhood Italian, serving simple, affordable River Café-style food, at a fraction of the starry Italian, a two floors contemporary trattoria with a reputation for fresh pasta, charcoal grilling, and gorgeous tarts. If it wasn't for the London buses and traffic outside you could even think you are in some trattoria in Italy.

They both loved its big bold flavours from great ingredients presented in a simple non-pretentious manner.

"Lunchtimes are calmer usually" Paola said, looking around perplexed.

"Sugar, I forgot: it's the pre-Gunners home game rush from the champagne-socialist-city types-Arsenal supporters".

"What are you like? Champagne socialists? PS: one of them is actually looking at you. Don't turn, he is coming over".

I guess boy meets girl meets boy is not much different at twenty, thirty or forty.
And so he came over, Mr. Champagne Socialist. Cute.

The Champagne Socialist was spending Christmas with Gabrielle and her family. She really liked how family oriented he was, and he was getting along really well with her mother which was a definite plus.

They had lunch with his children on Christmas Eve at his favourite restaurant, Le Boudin Blanc; a French restaurant located a short walking distance from Green Park tube station and the main road, a big family affair.

. . .

The smell of bacon and eggs wafted through the air. Gabrielle breathed in the aroma.

"The neighbours are having breakfast," she thought. She took a sip of her now warmish coffee.

Food, so many memories linked to food.

"I miss eating out ".

The Champagne Socialist was a foodie himself, only the best restaurants would do, Michelin starred mostly.

We had been at Le Boudin Blanc several times before, for lunch, dinner, after drinks, etc… and I loved it each and every time (and the extremely generous portions).

As soon as you venture down Trebeck Street you are transported in charming and picturesque alleyways – an oasis of calm amidst the hustle and bustle of city life, where leisurely business lunches are *de riguer* together with some people watching - literally speaking if you sit outside on the pavement.

Watching the world go by with nice food and wine is one of the best past-times. "God, I miss eating out".

"*Pour moi, Moules marinières à la crème et Confit de joues de porc, Jésus de Morteau, poitrine de porc fumée et cassoulet de haricots coco si vous plait*", Gabrielle said to the waiter, in French of course.

The lunch went swimmingly well, the service was excellent with perfect timing both for serving/clearing and giving enough attention to the diners but not too much to feel intrusive.

The evening was equally as glorious: Christmas Carols by Candlelight at the Royal Albert Hall followed by midnight Mass - a Christmas tradition for Gabrielle and her mum. The Champagne Socialist fitted in so well.

NOTE TO SELF: REMEMBER TO CHECK IF SOME RESTRICTIONS WILL BE LIFTED FOR THIS CHRISTMAS.

They exchanged gifts at midnight. Gabrielle opened her gift from CS: a chunky silver vintage bracelet with Murano glass. A quirky creation meant to appear bohemian and crafty, despite being so obviously expensive.

Everything he wore was designer, the type of clothes that have no label, simple but you have to mortgage a house to buy them. And he was buying in bulk.

Obviously so him. Obviously not Gabrielle. At all.

She remembered seeing it when they were browsing shops in Covent Garden looking for presents for his daughter and his dizzy sister.

"You don't like it, do you?" mum whispered after he had left the room. Gabrielle raised her eyebrows with a faint smile.

Mum still wears it all the time, she loves it.

. . .

It had taken some time for Gabrielle to realise that how she ultimately saw herself had governed her life.

She wanted change, She needed change. She needed to change.

Sometimes it takes a great emergency or crisis to delve deep and discover how much more you can do. Or should do. She was not afraid to make big choices: she left her big corporate job in the middle of the pandemic, and now taking her time to figure out what she really wanted.

She started to treat her body and herself with love and kindness, no more torture and self-flagellation with super hard schedules. Nothing to prove now.

Émile Coué talked about the power of self-suggestion and Gabrielle had been on working on just that. Like a method actor, she had fully immersed herself in her new character, finally releasing her mental shackles.

She was disciplined and committed. To herself. Until her new identity becomes part of her. Until it becomes her.

Everything can change, just like that.

If Covid-19 has taught her anything, it's that you can't put your life on hold and wait for the future. The road called "someday" leads to a town called "nowhere".

The happily ever after can be hers. Everything and everyone you meet is really just you.

And everything did change, one day, just like that ...

. . .

Gabrielle had ventured further out for her walk, further than the usual Islington confinement. She lost track of time and space listening to a podcast and her affirmations; she walked, and walked , and walked.

Down St John's road towards St Paul's.

She could see St Paul's from afar, standing tall, majestic, like a beacon. She remembered how much she loved attending the service there and listening to the Cathedral's Choir perform.

She was zigging and zagging from side to side to avoid the people she came across on the streets. Everyone was looking at each other suspiciously. Masks or no masks.

A few ambulances coming out of the gates at St. Bartholomew hospital.

The One New Change was deserted, "How depressing".

She had enjoyed walking around London like a tourist.

"Gosh, how long has it been now?" She had lived in London for twenty years now, never felt at home as much as here. Her heart was full of gratitude.

You can lose yourself in the streets of London, every day discover new nooks and crannies. Follow the River Thames, down to the Tate, or Borough Market.

"St Paul's will do today".

Gabrielle had been alone through the lockdown; her parents technically in her bubble but still living in the village, up

North.

"A bubble indeed".

She had a few trusted friends, her inner circle, but they all have their own family to think of. Gabrielle is the only single in the group. She had been single for over a year now. In the end she decided she was better off alone. At least until she had worked on herself and was sure about what she wanted and needed, truly deeply. Better off alone than with the wrong man.

She made un café allongé with a slash of double cream to take with her.

"Why did she do that?" She never ate or drank on the go. I guess not being able to stop at will had something to do with it. Or it was just fate.

She poured the hot fragrant mixture in her portable coffee cup and off she went on her long walk.

"I am a Goddess, I am a Queen", her affirmations playing in her ears. Gabrielle was taking her time, savouring every moment, every view.

Is there any other time but now? Amazing how much you can see when you are really looking.

She was absorbed in herself, finally standing in her own power as a fully embodied feminine woman, knowing that to be adored and be treated like a Goddess, you need to first know you ARE one. No need to act like a man anymore.

It had been a long journey, but she was finally arriving at her destination. She was ready to say "Yes"! to life in its entirety, comfortable in her body and her emotions, embracing ALL of herself.

She was lost in her thoughts, sipping her coffee as she turned around the corner ...

BANG! Ouch ...

The collision was surprisingly strong considering they were both just walking. Gabrielle had lost her balance but he was quick and promptly grabbed her by the waist to keep her from falling.

The coffee wasn't that lucky and splattered everywhere.

E-V-E-R-Y-W-H-E-R-E on her white dress.

"Life is not happening to me. Life is happening for me", she kept repeating in her mind looking down at the brown spots on her dress "Bummer, coffee stains and I'm nowhere near home".

They were so close now, he smelled real good.

"I am a Goddess ..." still playing in her ears.

"I am so so sorry" he said. She looked up , his piercing blue eyes shining, his dazzling smile peaking through the mask half down his chin. He looked firmly, steadily, straight into her soul.

. . .

"At least he is cute" Gabrielle thought "Thank you Universe".

"Are you OK?" he seemed truly mortified of what had happened.

"I'm OK, thank you. Not a big deal really. It is only coffee" playing it cool.

He was staring at her. She didn't know if to back up to keep some parvence of social distancing or hold the stare. Fuck it. Hold it.

She felt like getting closer instead. She didn't.

"Let me get your dress dry-cleaned for you" he offered.

"Dry cleaners are closed".

"OK, at least let me wash it for you".

"Really, it's only coffee, it's not a problem".

Gabrielle wondered if he was living in London or he got stuck here when lockdown started. He had a distinctive North American accent, New York she thought.

Judging, judging, stop it Gabri. Every Tom Dick and Harry lives in London; everybody has an accent here, including you.

"No, really, let me do this for you. I live just around the corner: I can wash your dress and have it ready back to you in a couple of hours. Perhaps even make you coffee while you wait. One that you can drink this time" he insisted.

Wait, did he just ask me back to his place and offered to wash my dress?

She squinted with her deep dark eyes staring into his and

said:

"Is this a cheap ploy to see me naked?"

"No, no, no, YES " ... mortified " No , no. I mean, it would be great but no".

She smiled profusely "I feel like I'm in a scene from the Vicar of Dibley: where is the camera?"

"What?" obviously not getting the reference.

"Sorry, British cultural reference. I'm kidding. I'm OK, seriously, no need to go through that much trouble. It is only coffee".

"I want to. I was hoping to spend more time with you ... perhaps a date tonight?"

The upfront American; she quickly glanced at his hands to see if there was any appearance of a wedding ring. Both hands, to be sure.

"Restaurants are closed too".

"I can cook". Dejavu.

"Social distancing?"

"I think we broke that rule already. We can eat alfresco, if that makes you feel better" he added.

"I don't really know you".

"I'm trying to remedy that" and sensing her reluctance "Can I have at least your number?"

Gabrielle was intrigued and totally attracted to him and so she did. He had just finished tapping her number into his mobile when her phone started ringing in her pocket.

"Are you going to get that? he asked.

"Pardon?"

"Your phone, are you going to answer it?"

"No, it's rude, I am talking to you. I can see who called me later".

"It's me".

"You can't be missing me already, I'm still here" she said grinning, gesticulating.

"I just want to make sure I have the right number. And you now have mine too" he was grinning too. "Are you sure I cannot convince you to have dinner with me tonight?"

"Not tonight".

"Another night then. Tomorrow?"

Gabrielle smiled. God this felt so good.

"I better go now", she smiled again, waved and started walking away.

She hadn't felt like this in a long time. Actually, ever. Her body was on fire, her spirit soaring.

"What just happened there?", she was walking on clouds.

It would have been the perfect exit had she not turned around to see if he was still there. But she couldn't help herself.

He was still there, standing still, looking. Smiling.

As she turned around the corner, her phone vibrated, a text:

"NOW, I <u>AM</u> MISSING YOU"
"THAT'S UNDERSTANDABLE," SHE REPLIED.

And just like that, that day, everything changed. A few months have passed by now and Gabrielle ...

Bang!

"Babe, I'm home".

The American, Mr Wonderful, peaked in the room to say hi, his sparkling blue eyes gazing at her. Soaking from the morning run. Water dripping on the floor.

"You are soaking wet".

"I'm going to have a shower," he said with a cheeky grin "want to join me?"

"Obviously," Gabrielle said.

I guess morning pages are done for today.

WITH LOVE
- GABRIELLE

EPILOGUE

We all have two images: the one that reflects from the mirror and the one WE see in the mirror. This, in turn, is determined by the paradigms that run our life (and mind).

But we were born free, without any preconceived ideas. Then, slowly but surely, the mental conditioning from our environment, our family, our education kicks in and, unfortunately, stacks up.

And this forms our subconscious Self-image.

Self-Image is our own limiting portable box. Our world and everything in it (career, body, money and relationships) reflect our mental attitude toward ourselves.

It's the ultimate internal regulator: every time it looks like we are about to break free, it will bring us back to base like a thermostat.

. . .

Unless we review and update the image we have of ourselves, we will reach sooner or later the "temperature" we are comfortable in. Then Self-sabotage comes in. And there we start again.

Look around at every aspect of your life – THAT's your ceiling.

#SmashYourCeiling never sounded more appropriate...

Laura xxx

"OUR SELF-IMAGE, STRONGLY HELD,
ESSENTIALLY DETERMINES WHAT WE BECOME"
- DR MAXWELL MALTZ

DISCLAIMER

Gabrielle is a work of fiction.

Although its form is that of an autobiography through the pages of one diary, it is not one.

With the exception of public places and the pandemic, any resemblance to persons living or dead is coincidental. Space and time have been rearranged to suit the convenience of the book, memory has its own story to tell.

The opinions expressed are those of the characters and should not be confused with the author's.

AUTHOR'S NOTE

Thank you so much for reading *Gabrielle*.

I hope you enjoyed this novel as an escapist story, but perhaps you also glimpsed something beneath as you read. A review would be much appreciated as it helps other readers discover the story. Thanks.

If you sign up for my newsletter you'll be notified of give-aways, new releases and receive personal updates from behind the scenes of my business and books.

Go to www.thepeoplealchemist.com to get started.

Places in the book

I have set the story in real places in London and my beloved Islington, and in a modeled fictional seaside village in England for Gabrielle's backstory. You can see some of the places here:

- Le Boudin Blanc
- Camden Passage
- Canonbury Square and Gardens

- The Estorick Collection of Modern Art
- Islington Farmers Market
- The Mandarin Oriental Hotel
- One New Change
- Salut
- St Paul's Cathedral
- Trullo.

Bibliography

I read a lot of books as part of my research. Some of them together with other references include:

Psycho-Cybernetics - **Maxwell Maltz**
Self Mastery Through Conscious Autosuggestion - **Émile Coué**
The Artist Way - **Julia Cameron**.
Tools of Titans - **Tim Ferris**.

Midsomer Murders - British crime drama television series adapted from the novels in the *Chief Inspector Barnaby* book series (created by Caroline Graham). The series focuses on various murder cases that take place within small country villages across the fictional English county of Midsomer.

Keeping up Appearances - British sitcom starring Patricia Routledge as the eccentric snob Hyacinth Bucket. It broadcast from 1990 to 1995.

The Vicar of Dibley - British sitcom starring Dawn French as the Vicar of the rural parish of Dibley, It made its debut in 1994.

Printed in Great Britain
by Amazon